THE MAN WITH THE DANCING EYES

By Sophie Dahl

Pictures By Annie Morris

BLOOMSBURY

Published by Bloomsbury, New York and London
Distributed to the trade by Holtzbrinck Publishers

Cataloging-in-Publication Data is available from the Library of Congress

ISBN 1-58234-342-X

First U.S. edition 2003

2 4 6 8 10 9 7 5 3 1

Designed by William Webb
Printed and bound in Italy by Artegrafica S.p.A, Verona

For the Shaffer

household with huge

love and gratitude

S.D.

In the golden half-light of a midsummer's evening, the sort where any kind of magic can occur, and often does, in the midst of a party held in a wild and rambling garden, stood Pierre, teetering on highly unsuitable heels, surrounded by a symphony of overripe roses.

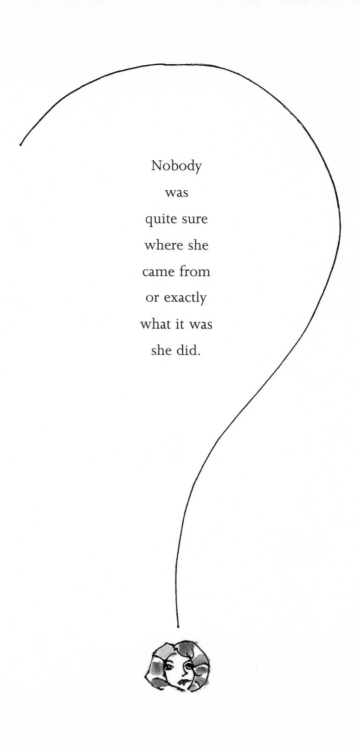

Nobody

was

quite sure

where she

came from

or exactly

what it was

she did.

'She has a past, that one,'
they would
mutter
excitedly,

as she loped by, gangly
as a baby giraffe,
green eyes flashing,
a whisper of a smile
playing on her lips.

In actuality Pierre had no dark secret,

nor was she the mistress of some faraway king.

She was simply rather shy and private.

Her birth and name were
the result of an unlikely
liaison between a bumbling
botanist and a ravishing yet
distant Italian soprano, who
found themselves stranded,
away from their native lands,
on a strange electric night.
Amidst the linen sheets
of the Pierre Hotel, as a
fearful storm raged outside,
our heroine was conceived
in the great city of New York.

She spent her childhood in a tall imposing house in Belgravia - alone, but for a host of homely nannies who adored her.

Her summers were spent in a crumbling *palazzo* outside Rome named the Villa Splendida, and her youth passed sweetly, solitary and uninterrupted, until either parent, filled with remorse or longing, would arrive to bewildering fanfare and sweep her off to exotic climes for a week or two.

Mostly she was happiest sitting on top of the Aga, her small nose firmly buried in a book.

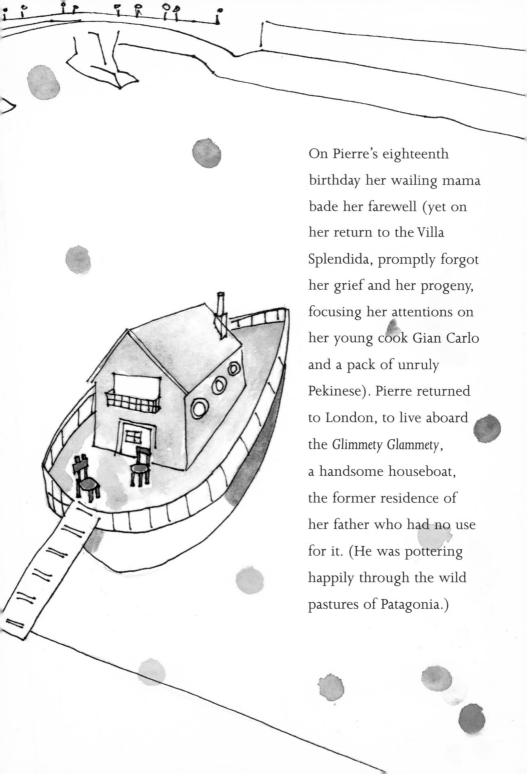

On Pierre's eighteenth birthday her wailing mama bade her farewell (yet on her return to the Villa Splendida, promptly forgot her grief and her progeny, focusing her attentions on her young cook Gian Carlo and a pack of unruly Pekinese). Pierre returned to London, to live aboard the *Glimmety Glammety*, a handsome houseboat, the former residence of her father who had no use for it. (He was pottering happily through the wild pastures of Patagonia.)

As her appetite for books had become voracious, it was with joy that she went to work for Beaney Esquire Rare Books on the King's Road, spending her days immersed in the yellowing pages of the classics. Mr Beaney was tender-hearted, stout and a bit of an old soak, truth be told. He owned a lurcher named Sampson, smelt of tweed, tobacco and starched linen, and every day at one o'clock sharp he would have his ritual lunch, a pint of Guinness and a teacup of Jameson's.

It was at his annual
fancy-dress party (great
figures of literature,
1850-1930), held in
the aforementioned
garden of his dusty house
in Old Church Street, that
Pierre glanced into the
eyes of fate.

As the opening bars of her favourite Ella Fitzgerald
song began to play she tried to take a step forward,
only to find that she was firmly rooted to the
ground, anchored by her Christian Louboutin shoes.

She felt a tap on her shoulder and found herself staring into the most wicked and dancing eyes she'd ever seen.

'You appear to be sinking,'
remarked her future beloved (though neither of them knew this fact, or indeed each other).

'Oh it's you,'
she said, and turned a hundred shades of scarlet.

'It is,'
he replied, beguiled by her blush, and irrationally pictured her surrounded by a troop of bonny babies. (His.)

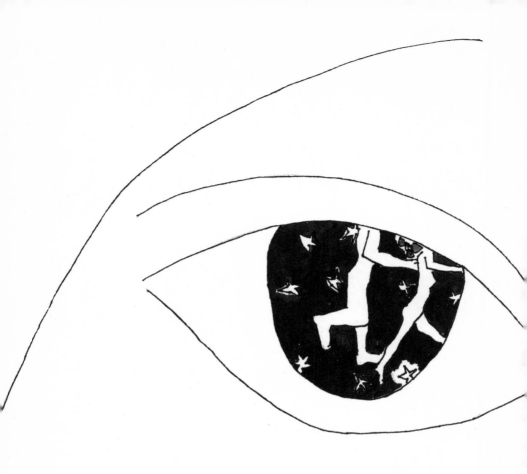

Pierre and the man with the dancing eyes (for this is what
she christened him) waltzed off into the night.
Under the stars they sat with a picnic (deftly conjured
up by Claridge's) drinking oceans of champagne.

They laughed and laughed, unable to eat,
for who can ... and who wants ... and who needs to ... EAT ...
when it's the beginning of love?

As the sun rose lazily above London, he kissed her on
Albert Bridge. She was filled with an inexplicable burst of joy,
although it could have been the champagne.

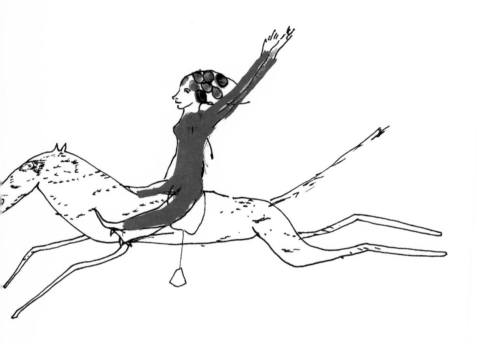

And there began a glorious affair.

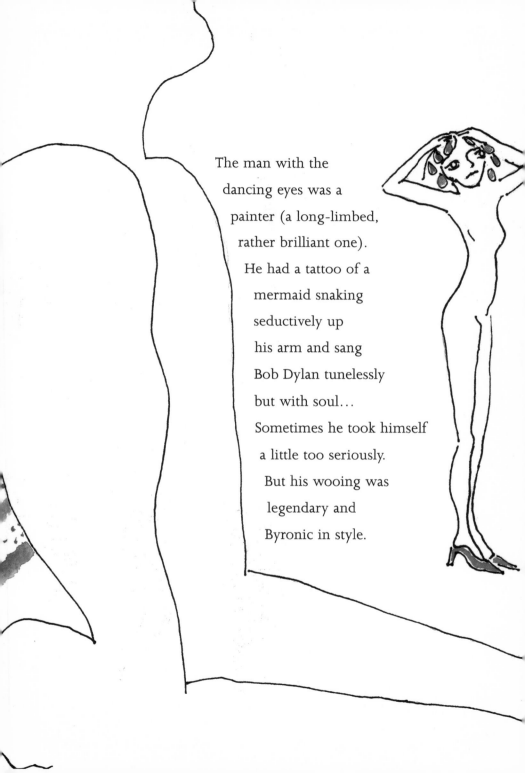

The man with the
dancing eyes was a
painter (a long-limbed,
rather brilliant one).
He had a tattoo of a
mermaid snaking
seductively up
his arm and sang
Bob Dylan tunelessly
but with soul…
Sometimes he took himself
a little too seriously.
But his wooing was
legendary and
Byronic in style.

Mr Beaney
was wildly
disapproving as
a pair of lovebirds,
followed by sea-horses,
interspersed with great
trails of sweet peas,
swept into the shop.
'This is a book shop, not a fecking
ark,' he exclaimed hotly. Pierre shrugged
innocently as Mr Beaney began to laugh,
and surrendered to the feeling of being
swept away by something
much bigger than she.

The man with the
dancing eyes took her to a
multitude of parties, and as they entered
a room, the feeling of her long pale hand
in his consumed him alive with pride.
'She's mine,' he wanted to sing
from the rooftops to anyone
that would listen.

He asked if he could paint her.
'I have found my muse,' he told his friends
excitedly. Pierre who had never been a muse
before found it thrilling lying supine wearing
nought but a mermaid's tail.

But to be a muse is a dangerous thing ...

As night, that faithful companion of lovers, broke the day, they sat

on the deck of the *Glimmety Glammety* in silence,

dangling their feet over the water.

'If you could live anywhere in the world, where would it be?'

the man with the dancing eyes asked.

'In a house surrounded by fields, probably in Italy,

with an Aga, four babies and a goat.'

'I see,' he replied, smiling steadily at her. Pierre was
utterly incandescent with happiness.
He sang 'I want you' by Bob Dylan like a lullaby every night.

The sweet peas continued
to arrive morning, noon
and night. Pierre loved,
loved, loved sweet peas,
and for the rest of her life
their scent became synonymous
with the pursuit of love.

The man with the dancing
eyes sketched her sleeping.
Then kissed her eyes till she
woke, whispering fervent
promises that skittered into her
half-awake ears like a dream.

That summer was filled with unceasing enchantment.
As day poured through the bedroom window, Pierre opened
her eyes to seven tiny men singing madrigals on the deck of
the *Glimmety Glammety*. Her beloved appeared at the bedroom door.
'I'm mad about you,' he proclaimed.
'Lucky, lucky me,' she said.
He later had a sweeping victory at Scrabble which
made her cross and distinctly ungracious.

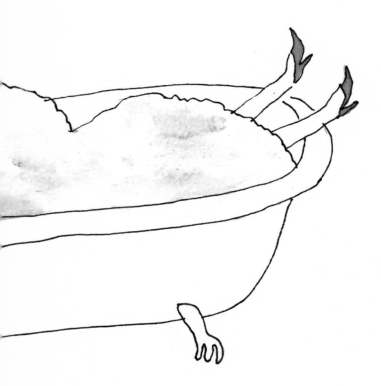

On those balmy lilting evenings he would read
T.S. Eliot to her as she lingered languid in a
bath overflowing with bubbles, pausing only to
feed her toast and Cooper's marmalade.

And yet and yet, for all the wonder, something, that intangible,

elusive something, was not quite right. His admiration though

ardent seemed to turn with the tides and Pierre felt oddly afraid.

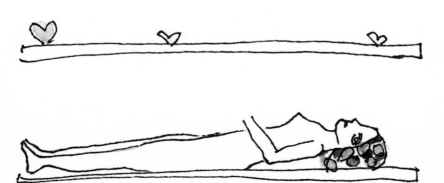

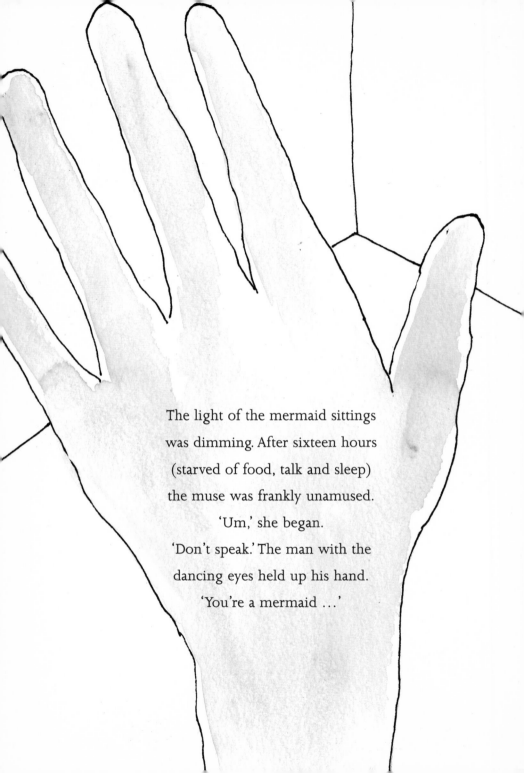

The light of the mermaid sittings
was dimming. After sixteen hours
(starved of food, talk and sleep)
the muse was frankly unamused.
'Um,' she began.
'Don't speak.' The man with the
dancing eyes held up his hand.
'You're a mermaid ...'

'I am not a mermaid,' Pierre shouted. 'I'm a girl
and I don't exist only in your imagination.
I'm here now. I'm real.'
'Keep still,' said the man
with the dancing eyes
with gritted teeth.
'You are IMPOSSIBLE,'
Pierre cried
and tripped
out of
the
door,
her tail
following
forlornly
behind
her.

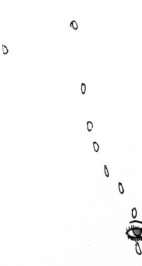

One rainy, doom Sunday
evening as they lay side
by side, Pierre asked,
dizzy and dazed, and
filled with a feeling of
imminent dread,
'Do you think you'll
always love me a bit?'
'Always a bit,'
he said quietly.
Oh how she loathed,
loathed, loathed rainy
Sunday evenings
with a passion.

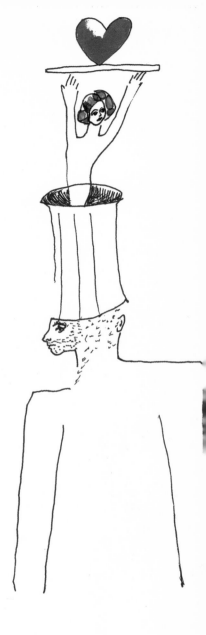

Alas, as it's been said, all good things
must end (WHY?). As summer turned
into a weary autumn he committed an
indiscretion that tore her in two.
Foolish foolish man.

It was a treachery she couldn't bear
and she decided to go some place, any
place, that didn't have him in it.

She told Mr Beany of her plan one late
September afternoon, and the slant of her
shoulders, and her eyes full of wretched-
ness, made him howl with abandon.
'Come back soon, my darling,'
he sobbed, pressing a first edition
of *The House of Mirth*
into her hand.

Even the sea-horses managed
to look morose; quite a feat
for a sea-horse.

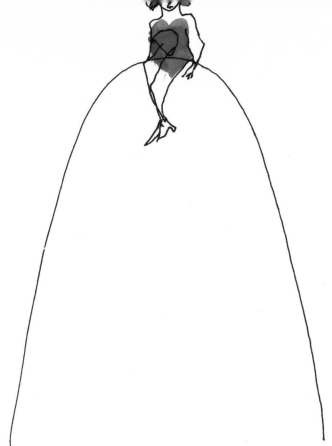

The man with the dancing eyes telephoned

on the eve of her departure.

'I can't tell you where I'm going,'

she told him,

'for I don't quite know myself.

Perhaps I'll join the sisterhood.'

He laughed dispiritedly.

'Sister Pierre, what will

the name of your

Order be?'

'My Order shall be called
the Convent of the Bleeding Heart
and Undeniable Compassion.'

A pause.
'Goodbye.'

Pierre packed up her bags, and left
in a flurry post the demise of her
tragic affair. Her heart felt as though
it had been stung by ten thousand
angry wasps. Her destination: the
city of her conception.

And there before her lay New York in all of its glittering, sprawling glory.

Pierre was struck by a pang of terror as she surveyed the grand city. 'I am on an adventure,' she said firmly to the wind. A pair of brazen New York seagulls hooted with derision as they flew past.

'Oh piss off,' said she, and feeling immediately better she skipped across the Brooklyn Bridge doing a jaunty two-step …

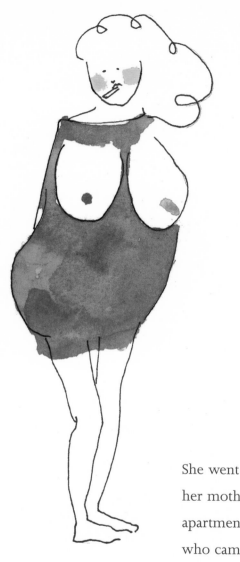

She went to live with a friend of her mother named Blue in a tiny apartment on West 4th Street. Blue, who came from New Orleans, had scarlet nails, a penchant for jazz musicians and a smoker's cough. She liked to drink Lapsang Souchong day and night.

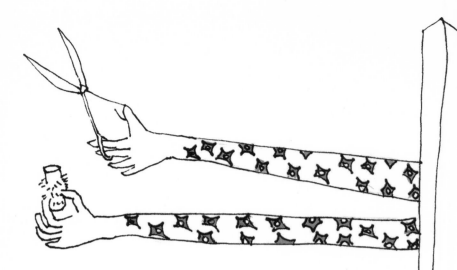

The apartment was above a hairdresser's which had
a sign that read 'Hubert ... Hair', and when she
went out at night, often with hair unkempt, a tall
and spindly man would run after her with heated
rollers, shouting mournfully, 'Just a quick set.'
She presumed this was Hubert.

She acquired a mongrel with loyal eyes and named him Froggy.

Froggy loved Pierre and at night he would curl sweetly at her feet looking quizzical yet understanding as she wept.

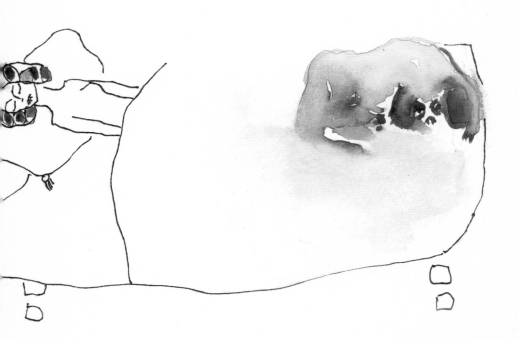

Falling into exhausted sleep she
dreamt of sailors with sad eyes,
singing low shanty songs to
disinterested mermaids, and
sometimes of him. Waking furious,
alone, berating her subconscious
for letting him invade her dreams.

'How dare you,'
she'd whisper to
no one in particular.

Pierre became an artist's model for a
secretive painter named Mr Chin. His
draughty studio was filled with an almost
reverential silence, but for the comforting
hiss of the ancient radiators, which
allowed her feverish mind to be still. Mr
Chin draped her in a swathe of dusty
Shanghai silk and taught her to tango. She
taught him sailor's knots and how to drink
tequila without grimacing – AN ART. He
told her she was a Renaissance
woman.

She decided it was
time for the snip
and entrusted her
locks to Hubert-the-Hair
who lived downstairs.

THIS WAS A MISTAKE.

'New hair, new man,'
said Hubert-the-Hair brightly.

'I hope the man isn't as
ghastly as the hair,'
muttered Pierre darkly.

Although his scissors were
never to touch her head
again, they became
quite inseparable.

Valiant attempts were made to forget the dancing-eyed man, and Pierre endured a series of dismal dinners with a crowd of unsuitable suitors who were hopelessly encouraged by her air of melancholy and indifference.

Floral tributes poured in constantly to the delight of Hubert.

'Another bouquet of red roses,'
Hubert-the-Hair called dramatically.
'Are you sure no sweet peas?'
came the despondent reply.
'Quite, quite sure.'
'Ohhh, I'm trying to be grateful but ...'
'I know,'
Hubert said understandingly.

Arriving home after these dinners, sitting in her nightdress, wracked by a longing so painful it felt like a sickness, she wrote letters to the man with the dancing eyes, which were never sent …

One night she sat on her fire-escape and a taxi pulled up outside playing 'I want you' so loudly that for one delicious heady minute she thought he had come to get her.

As the taxi drove off, she climbed back through the bedroom window cursing her romantic heart and bumped her head. 'Bloody bloody Bob Dylan,' she said, and burst into tears. Froggy howled in unison.

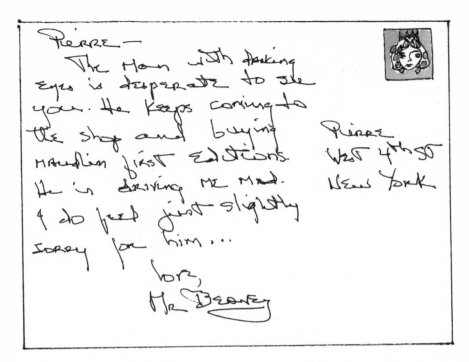

Pierre —
The Man with parking
Eyes is desperate to see
you. He keeps coming to
the shop and buying
maudlin first editions.
He is driving me mad.
I do feel just slightly
sorry for him ...
           love,
        Mr Beaney

Pierre
W25 4th St
New York.

Postcards flew through the letterbox. In Mr Beaney's spidery hand.

Pierre wrote back.

Darling Mr B,
Don't.
Love Pierre

But her heart leapt a little. 'CEASE. NOW,' she instructed it ...

Over Lapsang Souchong one morning, Blue sighed
wearily and coughed with passion.

Reaching for another Sobranie she said, 'Look, why don't
you just marry someone rich and boring, deary.'

'Alas, I don't think I could,' replied Pierre glumly.
'Hmph,' Blue snorted.

Blue was what is known as On the Shelf.

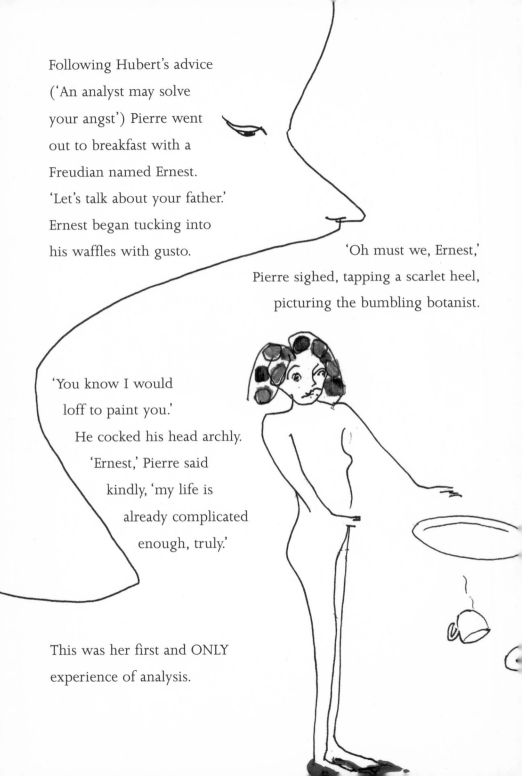

Following Hubert's advice
('An analyst may solve
your angst') Pierre went
out to breakfast with a
Freudian named Ernest.
'Let's talk about your father.'
Ernest began tucking into
his waffles with gusto.

'Oh must we, Ernest,'
Pierre sighed, tapping a scarlet heel,
picturing the bumbling botanist.

'You know I would
loff to paint you.'
He cocked his head archly.
'Ernest,' Pierre said
kindly, 'my life is
already complicated
enough, truly.'

This was her first and ONLY
experience of analysis.

She also met a group of merry
Italians and they spent the
evening in Brooklyn getting
hopelessly drunk on zambuca.

She beat them at poker and they
laughed when she said
straight-faced:

'Are you in the Mafia?'

They were of course; and were all called Frankie.

MONDAY

When she was not posing for Mr Chin she would pace the streets

TUESDAY

of Manhattan, often finding herself in the Mummy Room at the

WEDNESDAY

Metropolitan Museum of Art.

THURSDAY

This became one of her favourite haunts.

FRIDAY

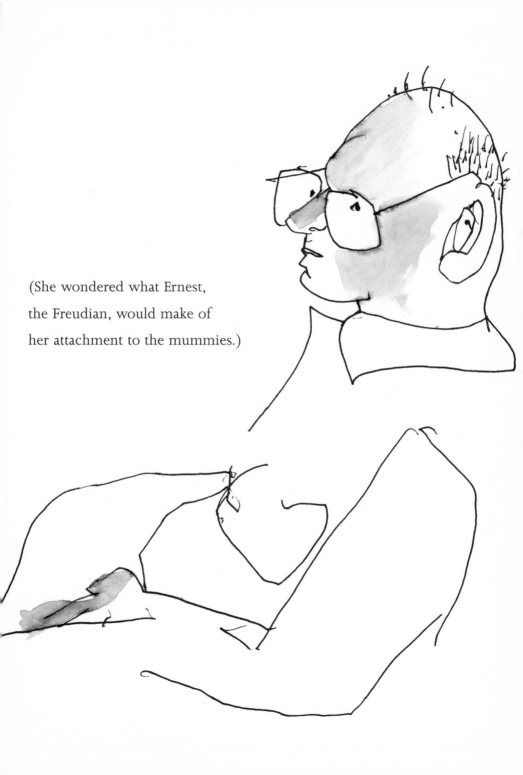

(She wondered what Ernest,
the Freudian, would make of
her attachment to the mummies.)

On Saturdays
Hubert and Pierre
would breakfast at
the Mercer Hotel. A treat.
They decided that
when they were
VERY RICH
indeed they would
live there and throw witty,
lavish lunch parties.
'Oh how I love the Mercer,'
Pierre sighed,
surreptitiously passing
Froggy half of her bagel.

When funds were low they went
to Canal Street and bought Chinese
slippers, paper butterflies,
and yards of ribbons.

Walking home from Mr Chin's as a blustery dusk
fell and the city surged around her, Froggy trotting
by her side, Pierre was struck by a wave of tenderness
for New York.

She burst through the door of West 4th Street.
'Blue, I love it here,' she said with great ceremony.

'FOR NOW,' Blue replied dolefully.

Pierre kissed her round cheeks and they danced to
Dean Martin till three with the Frankies.

Christmas was nearly intolerable. Hubert
had fallen in love and gone to Boca
Raton. Blue went into decline and locked
herself in her bedroom, great wafts of
smoke billowing under the door.

''Tis the season to be jolly,'
Pierre reasoned.

'Leave me to my misery,'
Blue howled.

She came out later and
demolished a plate of
mince pies with fervour.

The unsuitable suitors' roses sat: a fat smug line in the corridor,
banished from her bedroom.

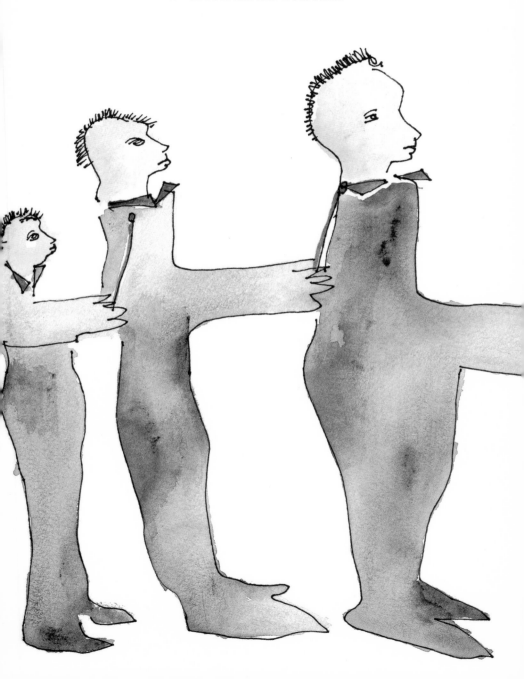

Yet despite the floral
embargo, on February
the 14th, a single
sweet pea drifted like
bindweed through her
window and came to
rest by her sleeping
cheek: UNNOTICED.

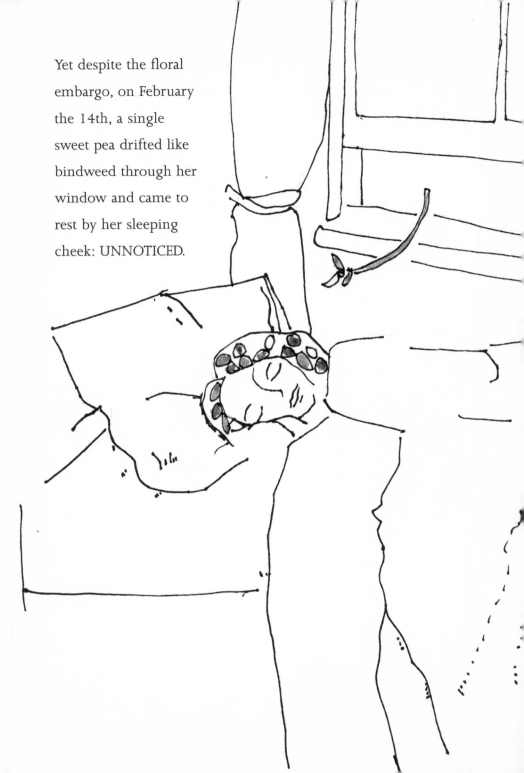

'Something is about to happen,'
Blue said broodingly into her Lapsang Souchong.
'I can feel it in my waters.'

Pierre thought privately that she didn't really
want to know about Blue's waters.

'I'm off to the
Met to see
my mummies, Blue,'
Pierre called later.

'Marvellous,'
Blue croaked,
waving her
Sobranie.

Pierre was whisked up town in a taxi
at breakneck speed, the Ella Fitzgerald song
that she had danced to at Mr Beaney's party
playing loudly, promptly followed by a loud
rendition of 'I want you'.

How very curious,
Pierre thought, looking at the driver suspiciously.

'I hope you have someone's love to keep you warm,'
said the driver as she got out.

'Yes,' replied Pierre crisply.
'My dog's. Goodbye.'

'What do I care, I've got
your love to keep me
warm,' Pierre sang.
'Except I don't la la la.'

It was cold as only New York can be in
February. The wind stung her face and
whipped her hair about her ears.

She sat on the steps of the Metropolitan
and watched 5th Avenue,
Froggy on her lap.

'Oh Froggy,' she said, quite overwhelmed by
nostalgia and tiredness and longing.

She thought for a moment she saw Mr Beaney
weaving through traffic looking decidedly
shifty. The thought dismissed she resumed
her bleak thoughts which had become rather
self-indulgent.

Pierre felt a tap on her shoulder and found
herself looking into the most wicked and
dancing eyes she had ever seen.

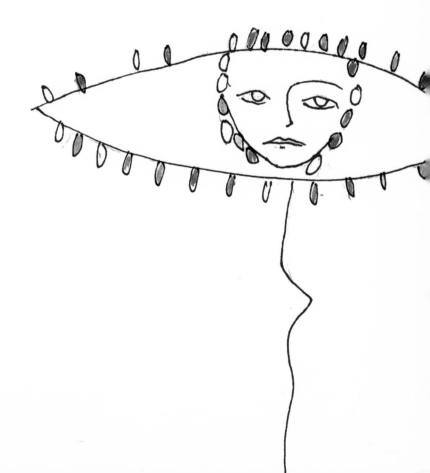

'Oh it's you,' she said.

'It's me. I love you. I want to live in Italy,
have an Aga, four babies and a goat.
I can't stand to be without you.'

'You'll have to go away, because I've given you up
for Lent and I've met a bullfighter from Seville,'
she said.

'Oh,' he said gravely.

There was long silence.

'I haven't really,' she said, suddenly shy.

'I love you, it's dreadful and grim,

I've tried so hard not to but I just do.'

'Lucky, lucky me,' he said,
and swept her into his arms like
she had never left them.

THE END